GW00870531

FROM
LIBRARY SERVIC

For Skye

A CIP catalogue record for this title is available from the British Library.

ISBN: 9781786126146 (paperback)
ISBN: 9781786126153 (hardback)
ISBN: 9781786126160 (eBook)

www.austinmacauley.com

First Published (2016)
Austin Macauley Publishers Ltd.
25 Canada Square
Canary Wharf
London
E14 5LQ

Acknowledgments

I would like to thank my family for their support and encouragement. Also a heartfelt thank you to Austin Macauley for turning my dream into reality.

About the Author

Lilli Sutherland is a first time children's author. With her creative mind and artistic flair, she wrote this tale. Born is St. Vincent & the Grenadines and raised in the UK, Lilli's passion for nature and animals is reflected in her book.

Jasper at Plumrose Farm

Lilli Sutherland

This book belongs to ....

Plumrose Farm was a fun place to be.
Goats, sheep, ducks, a cockerel, a mother hen with her five chicks and an old donkey named Davey, lived there.

It was Easter-time and the farm was a very noisy place. In the kitchen, Rosie, the farmer's wife, was busy making coconut tarts. Through the window she could hear the young lambs bleating, chicks chirping, ducklings quacking and puppies whimpering. It sounded like a dawn chorus with the animals singing their songs.

In a sty nearby, was a mummy pig, called a sow, with her eight piglets all snoozing in the hot tropical sunshine.
A fat tabby cat was also relaxing, watching her three mischievous kittens chase insects.
An enormous mango tree provided some cool shade over the sty.

The smallest kitten was called Jasper. He had stripey black and brown fur with a black patch around his left eye. He was very cute and looked almost like a tiger cub.

Jasper was a nervous kitten, easily frightened.
He never strayed too far from his mummy and wished
he was brave like his brothers.

He was scared of
tiny spiders,
dainty ladybirds,
lazing lizards,
squiggly tadpoles,
creepy-crawly
caterpillars and
wriggly earthworms.

One day Jasper was scampering about chasing a pretty blue butterfly.
But before long he had strayed too far from his mummy and was lost.

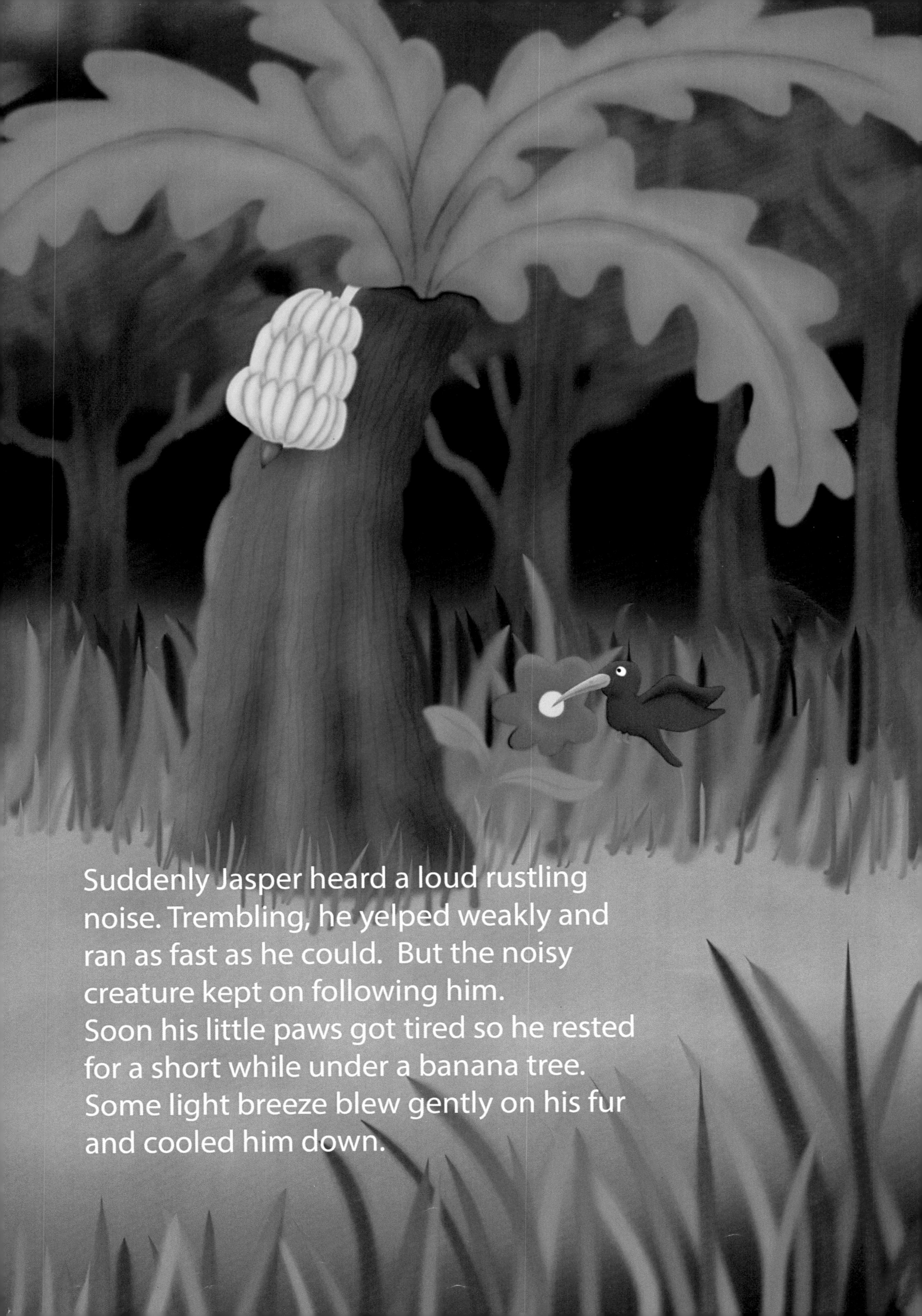

Suddenly Jasper heard a loud rustling noise. Trembling, he yelped weakly and ran as fast as he could. But the noisy creature kept on following him.
Soon his little paws got tired so he rested for a short while under a banana tree. Some light breeze blew gently on his fur and cooled him down.

By now Jasper was feeling very sad because he missed his mummy and two playful brothers.
Jasper tried really, really hard to be brave.
How he wished he could face the creature and fight it.
He wanted to **GRRH** at it!

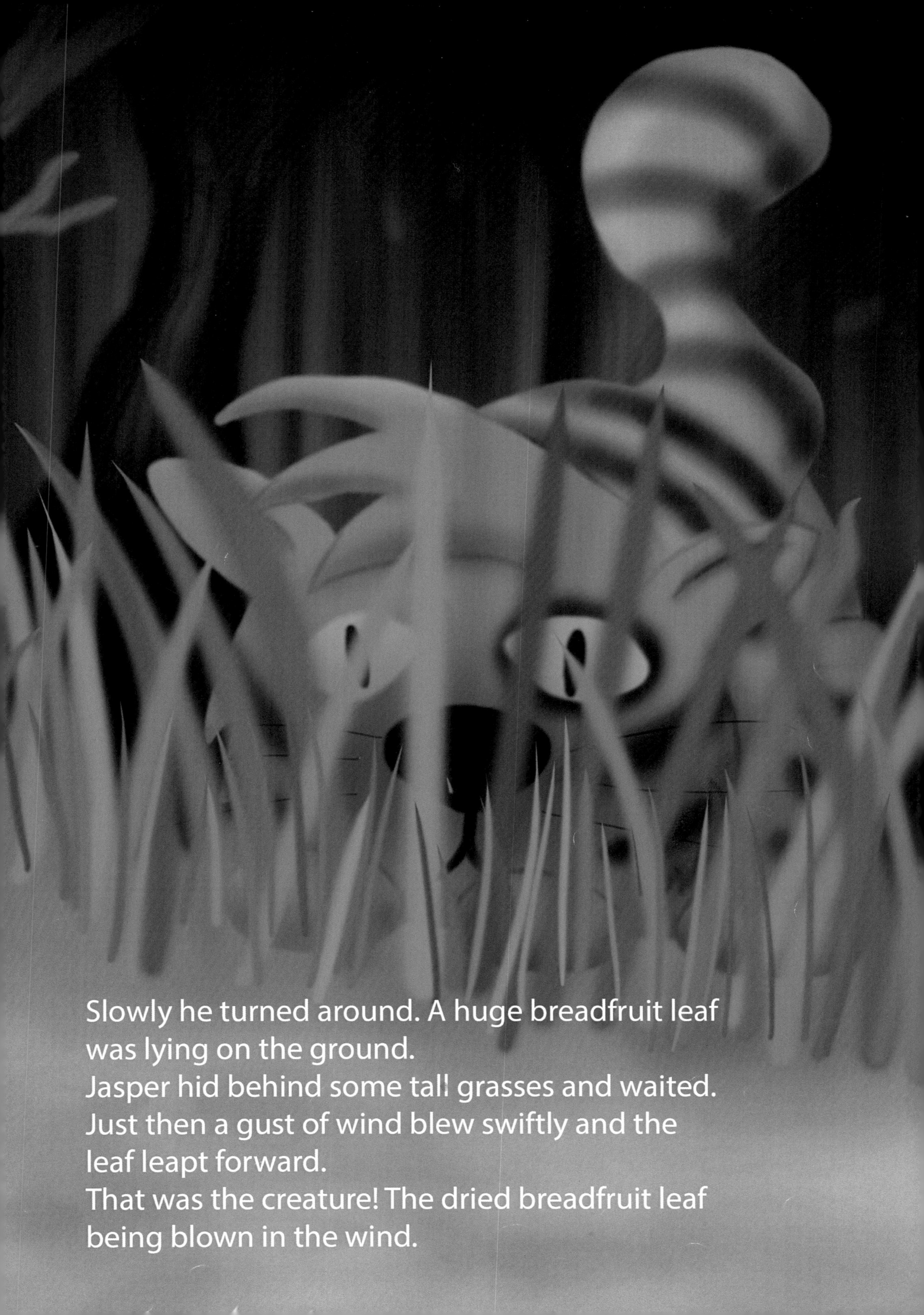

Slowly he turned around. A huge breadfruit leaf was lying on the ground.
Jasper hid behind some tall grasses and waited.
Just then a gust of wind blew swiftly and the leaf leapt forward.
That was the creature! The dried breadfruit leaf being blown in the wind.

Phew! Jasper was so relieved but now he was lost. He couldn't find his way home. He felt lonely. He missed all the animals on Plumrose Farm.

He dreamed of snuggling up
with his mummy.
Not long after, a cheerful
grasshopper named Georgie
hopped into the tall grasses.
He heard Jasper crying.

Georgie showed Jasper the way back to Plumrose Farm.
Jasper was very happy to be home again.
But his brothers laughed when Georgie told them what the creature was.

On that day Jasper decided to grow brave and strong.
He wasn't going to be a scaredy cat anymore!

The End

What is a Breadfruit?

Breadfruit, grown on a large tree, is a big starchy vegetable that can sometimes be the size of a football. It can be cooked and eaten in a similar way to a potato, and is often roasted outdoors on an open fire.

What is a Plum Rose?

Grown on a massive, green leafy tree, the plum rose is a red, juicy, pear-shaped fruit. It has white flesh that tastes and smells like delicate rose petals, and is loved by children and adults alike.

What are Coconut Tarts?

Made from dough and shaped like pasties, coconut tarts are filled with cooked, red-dyed, sweetened, freshly grated coconut and baked in the oven. When I was young, they were a special treat at Easter. One of my fondest childhood memories was of my grandmother making them - they were yummy!